OWL WANTS TO SHARE AT
MOONLIGHT SCHOOL

First published 2015
by Nosy Crow Ltd
The Crow's Nest, 10a Lant Street,
London SE1 1QR
www.nosycrow.com

ISBN 978 0 85763 484 9 (HB)
ISBN 978 0 85763 485 6 (PB)

Nosy Crow and associated logos
are trademarks and/or registered
trademarks of Nosy Crow Ltd.

FOR
LINDSEY FRASER
S.P.

FOR MORAG
A.P.

A CIP catalogue record for this book is
available from the British Library.

Printed in China

Papers used by Nosy Crow are made
from wood grown in sustainable forests.

1 3 5 7 9 8 6 4 2 (HB)
1 3 5 7 9 8 6 4 2 (PB)

OWL WANTS TO SHARE AT
MOONLIGHT SCHOOL

SIMON PUTTOCK
Illustrated by ALI PYE

nosy crow

This is Miss Moon's Moonlight School
for all the wee small creatures of the night.

The night bell had already rung,
  and Bat
    and Cat
      and Owl
        and Mouse
      were all ready and waiting.
        But somebody was missing
          and that somebody was . . .

...Miss Moon!
Suddenly, she
stepped out of the
crayon cupboard.
It was drawing time!

"I like drawing,"
said Mouse.

"Me too!" said Bat.

"And me!" said Cat.

"I do like drawing sometimes," said Owl, "but only when I'm good at it."

"Tonight," said Miss Moon, "you will all be wonderful. I want you each to draw a FAVOURITE night-time THING."

Mouse put up her paw IMMEDIATELY. "I will draw a dark and glinty SEA!"

Bat put up her wing. "I will draw a dark and whispery TREE!"

"I," said Cat, "will draw a BEE!"

"But bees are not night-time things," said Bat.

"Mine is," said Cat, "and it is dark and MYSTERIOUS, too!"

"What LOVELY ideas,"
said Miss Moon.
"Now, Owl, what would
you like to draw?"

Owl needed more deciding
time, so, "I am going to draw
a secret," he said.

Mouse and Cat and Bat
all chose their crayons
and started drawing.

Owl was still deciding.

"Is everything all right,
Owl dear?" asked Miss Moon.

Owl looked up at Miss Moon.
He THOUGHT he had
an idea, and then . . .

. . . he knew EXACTLY what to draw!

Owl hurried to the crayon pot, but all the nice night colours were taken. Poor Owl.

He did want his picture to be JUST RIGHT.

"I'm sure the others will share with you when they've finished," said Miss Moon.

But Cat and Bat and Mouse
NEEDED all the night-time colours,
and simply could not, WOULD not share!

"I am not finished,"
Cat explained.

"I am not finished
either," said Bat.

"I expect I shall not be finished
for AGES," said Mouse.

Owl would have to make do with
DAYTIME colours!

Feeling very worried indeed,
he began to draw . . .

Miss Moon watched to see how everyone was getting on. She was very impressed with Mouse's sea and Bat's tree and Cat's dark mysterious bee. Then she looked at Owl's picture.

"How lovely!" said Miss Moon.

Owl blushed.

Mouse and Cat and Bat
all hurried to take a look.
Owl was drawing
a picture of . . .

". . . YOU, Miss Moon!" said Owl.
"But," said Bat, "Miss Moon does NOT have
BLUE-GREEN hair, and it is not curly, either!"

"She does
not have a
YELLOW hat,"
said Cat. "AND
her hats are
always pointy!"

"And Miss Moon
never wears STRIPY
frocks," said Mouse.
"Owl has drawn
Miss Moon
ALL WRONG!"

"I think Owl has made me look special and different," said Miss Moon. "I am not sure I will have my hair blue-green and curly, and I never do wear stripy frocks of any sort, but I might look rather dashing in that hat!"

And it was true. Owl had made Miss Moon look special and different, and lovely, too.

"You are clever, Owl!" said
Mouse and Bat and Cat.
Owl's picture had given
them all new ideas . . .

"We need to borrow your crayons, please," they said.

"All right," said Owl.
"But I haven't finished
my picture either."
(He had had a new idea, too!)
"Can I borrow the night-time
crayons, please?"

"You can use mine," said Mouse.
"And mine," said Bat.
"What will Owl draw now?"
Cat wondered.

Owl looked clever
and said nothing.

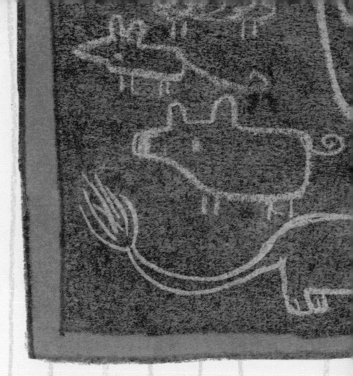

When drawing time was over,
it was time to admire everyone's
pictures properly.

Mouse's sea was
dark and glinty with
orange fishes.

Cat's bee was dark and
mysterious, but now it had
blue-green wings and an umbrella.

Bat's tree was dark
and whispery
with yellow birds.

But what had Owl drawn with
all the nice night-time colours?

"Oh Owl," said Miss Moon.
"How lovely! You've put us
ALL in your picture!
Now, I am thinking of
a night-time thing, too."

"Is it a teddy bear?"
asked Mouse.
Miss Moon shook her head.

"Is it a banana?" asked Cat.
Miss Moon shook her
head AGAIN.

"I bet it's a biscuit," said Bat.
"Biscuits are NICE,"
said Miss Moon, "but . . . no."

"I think it might be a flower," said Owl.

Miss Moon just smiled.

"None of you have guessed correctly so I will show you instead . . ."

. . . and she gave Owl and Bat
and Mouse and Cat
each a golden night-time star.